STAR WARS®

ATTACK OF THE CLONES™

A STORYBOOK ADAPTED BY
JANE MASON AND SARAH HINES-STEPHENS
BASED ON THE STORY BY
GEORGE LUCAS
AND THE SCREENPLAY BY
GEORGE LUCAS AND JONATHAN HALES

INTERIOR DESIGN BY IAIN R. MORRIS

RANDOM HOUSE 🏠 NEW YORK

SPECIAL THANKS TO THE FOLLOWING PEOPLE FOR THEIR WORK ON THIS BOOK.

AT LUCAS LICENSING:

Lucy Autrey Wilson, *Director of Publishing*
Sue Rostoni, *Managing Editor*
Iain R. Morris, *Art Editor*
Jonathan W. Rinzler, *Editor*
Chris Cerasi, *Editor*

AT RANDOM HOUSE CHILDREN'S BOOKS:

Alice Alfonsi, *Editorial Director*
Jason Zamajtuk, *Associate Art Director*
Kerry Milliron, *Brand Manager*
Artie Bennett, *Copy Chief*
Christopher Shea, Jenny Golub, Stephanie Finnegan,
  and Colleen Fellingham, *Copy Editors*
Milt Wackerow, Carol Naughton, *Production Managers*

www.randomhouse.com/kids

Official *Star Wars* Web Sites:
www.starwars.com
www.starwarskids.com

Library of Congress Control Number: 2001096261
ISBN: 0-375-81534-1
Printed in the United States of America
April 2002   10 9 8 7 6 5 4 3 2 1
First Edition

A LONG TIME AGO
IN A GALAXY FAR, FAR AWAY. . . .

THERE IS UNREST IN THE GALACTIC SENATE.
SEVERAL THOUSAND SOLAR SYSTEMS
HAVE DECLARED THEIR INTENTIONS
TO LEAVE THE REPUBLIC.

THIS SEPARATIST MOVEMENT,
UNDER THE LEADERSHIP OF COUNT DOOKU,
HAS MADE IT DIFFICULT FOR THE
LIMITED NUMBER OF JEDI KNIGHTS
TO MAINTAIN PEACE
AND ORDER IN THE GALAXY.

SENATOR AMIDALA,
THE FORMER QUEEN OF NABOO,
IS RETURNING TO VOTE ON THE CRITICAL ISSUE
OF CREATING AN ARMY OF THE REPUBLIC
TO ASSIST THE
OVERWHELMED JEDI . . .

Senator Padmé Amidala's Naboo Cruiser touched down safely on the landing platform. Three Naboo starfighters landed beside it.

"I guess I was wrong," remarked Captain Typho, the Senator's head of security. "There was no danger at all."

A female pilot, standing next to Typho, nodded in agreement. Nothing seemed out of the ordinary. But as the Senator and her handmaidens emerged from her ship, the platform was rocked by a huge explosion!

The Cruiser was blasted apart. Everyone near the ship was hurled to the ground. And the Naboo Senator lay on the platform, completely still.

The female pilot rushed to the motionless body. Kneeling, the pilot pulled off her helmet to reveal her identity: Padmé Amidala, the *real* Senator of Naboo.

"No!" Padmé cried, gathering the fallen young woman in her arms. But it was too late. Cordé, her bodyguard and decoy, had been killed.

Padmé was heartbroken, but there was no time to grieve. The danger was not over.

Later that day, Padmé traveled to the high towers of the Republic Executive Building. Inside, the head of the Senate, Chancellor Palpatine, was talking with several Jedi Masters.

Palpatine did not wish to see the Republic split in two. But the Jedi warned Palpatine to be careful. A wrong move could bring about a war with the Separatists, the group of solar systems threatening to leave the Republic. The Jedi were committed to protecting the Republic, but there were not enough of them to fight a war.

In the middle of their discussion, Padmé entered. After greeting everyone, she asked the Jedi if they knew who had tried to kill her.

"Our intelligence points to angry spice miners on the moons of Naboo," answered Jedi Master Mace Windu.

Padmé disagreed. "I think Count Dooku was behind it."

The Jedi were surprised. Dooku was an important leader in the Separatist movement—but he had once been a Jedi.

"It's not in his character to assassinate anyone," Mace insisted.

"In dark times nothing is what it appears to be," said Master Yoda. "But the fact remains, Senator, in grave danger you are."

Padmé was accustomed to danger and refused the offer of extra bodyguards—until Palpatine suggested an old friend.

"I will have Obi-Wan Kenobi report to you," Mace announced.

Padmé nodded. It would be good to see Obi-Wan again.

"Obi! Obi! Obi! Mesa sooo smilen to see'en yousa. Wahooooo!" Representative Jar Jar Binks could not contain his excitement. It had been ten years since he'd last seen Obi-Wan and his apprentice, Anakin Skywalker. Annie was no longer the little boy Jar Jar remembered. He'd grown into a strong young man.

"Shesa expecting yousa!" Jar Jar burbled as he led the Jedi into Padmé's quarters.

After greeting Obi-Wan, Padmé turned her eyes on Anakin. "My goodness, you've grown," she exclaimed.

"So have you . . . grown more beautiful, I mean . . . for a Senator, I mean," Anakin stammered.

"Oh, Annie, you'll always be that little boy I knew on Tatooine," Padmé said, making the Jedi apprentice blush. Then she turned to Obi-Wan and firmly warned him, "I don't need security, I need answers. I want to know who is trying to kill me."

Obi-Wan frowned. "We're here to protect you, Senator, not to start an investigation."

Anakin was anxious to impress Padmé. "We will find out who is trying to kill you, Padmé, I promise you!" he blurted out.

"We will do exactly as the Council has instructed," Obi-Wan corrected with a scowl, "and you will learn your place, young one."

Meanwhile, high above the bustling city planet, an armor-clad bounty hunter stood balanced on a ledge. Beside him stood a beautiful assassin.

"I hit the ship, but they used a decoy," the assassin said.

"We'll have to try something more subtle this time, Zam," the bounty hunter replied. "My client is getting impatient. Take these. . . . There can be no mistakes this time."

Zam Wesell accepted a tube filled with deadly, squirming kouhuns before turning toward her airspeeder.

She had failed to kill Senator Padmé Amidala the first time. But she would soon finish the job.

That night, while guarding Padmé, Obi-Wan and Anakin sensed something was wrong. A moment later, they burst through her bedroom door.

Poisonous kouhuns were slithering on Padmé's pillow only inches from her face! They reared back, hissing.

Anakin raced forward, his lightsaber raised. It hummed in the air, slicing the deadly creatures in half.

Padmé was safe. For now.

Suddenly, Obi-Wan spotted something outside the window—the Assassin Droid that had delivered the kouhuns!

Crashing through the window, he grabbed hold of the flying droid. The menacing droid sank under the weight of the Jedi.

Hanging on to it, Obi-Wan dangled hundreds of stories above the city as the Assassin Droid made its rapid retreat.

"Stay here," Anakin told Padmé.

After charging out of the building, Anakin jumped into an open airspeeder. He gunned the engine and took off toward the lines of traffic high above him.

Meanwhile, the droid tried to shake and shock Obi-Wan loose as it sped toward its employer, Zam Wesell.

"I have a bad feeling about this," Obi-Wan mumbled as he saw Zam take aim with her blaster rifle.

A blast struck the droid, and Obi-Wan was blown free. He plunged downward, falling more than fifty stories before landing on the rear of an airspeeder. After hauling himself into the passenger seat, he turned to the driver.

"What took you so long?" Obi-Wan asked.

"Oh, you know, Master, I couldn't find a speeder I really liked," Anakin joked as he raced across the spacelanes. Meanwhile, Zam jumped into her own airspeeder, trying to escape. Anakin, however, was an expert pilot, and he wasn't about to let her go!

Anakin steered sharply away from the spacelanes.

"Where are you going?!" Obi-Wan shouted.

"This is a shortcut," Anakin assured Obi-Wan. "I think."

Obi-Wan continued to bellow at his apprentice. But Anakin did not stay to listen. He leaped out of the airspeeder.

Using the Force, he safely dropped dozens of stories and landed on the roof of Zam's airspeeder!

With his lightsaber, he cut through the speeder to reach her. But Zam was ready. She fired, knocking Anakin's lightsaber out of his hand.

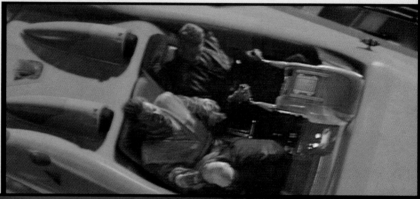

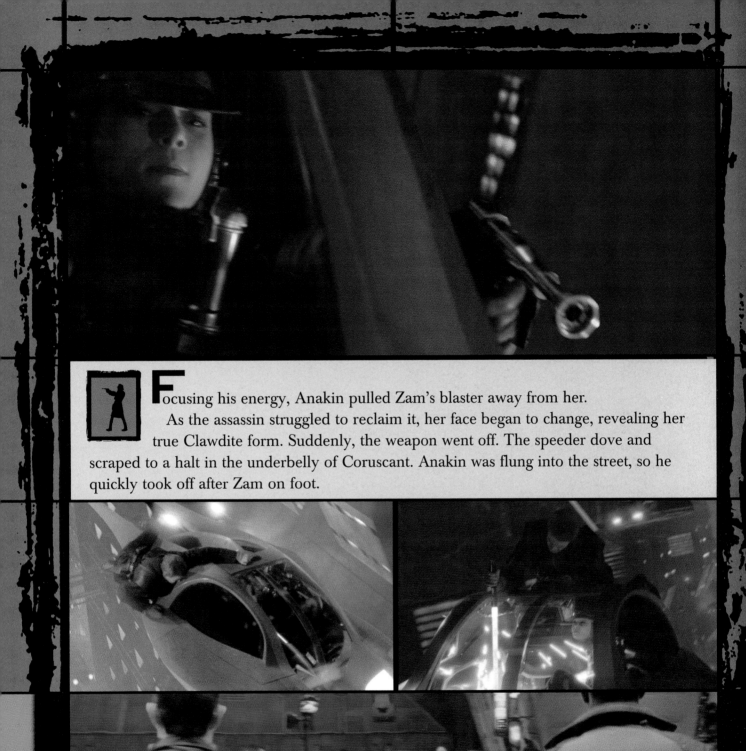

ocusing his energy, Anakin pulled Zam's blaster away from her.

As the assassin struggled to reclaim it, her face began to change, revealing her true Clawdite form. Suddenly, the weapon went off. The speeder dove and scraped to a halt in the underbelly of Coruscant. Anakin was flung into the street, so he quickly took off after Zam on foot.

Obi-Wan caught up to Anakin as he was about to follow Zam into a seedy nightclub. Obi-Wan held out his apprentice's lightsaber. He had snagged it as it flew out of Zam's speeder.

"This weapon is your life," said Obi-Wan. "Don't lose it again."

Anakin nodded. "I'm sorry, Master."

After taking back his lightsaber, Anakin entered the club with Obi-Wan. They searched the sea of alien faces. Anakin did not sense the blaster that was leveled at his Master's back. Luckily, Obi-Wan did.

With a single lightsaber slash, he severed Zam's arm, and the chase was over. The Jedi carried the wounded assassin into an alley. "Who hired you?" Anakin demanded.

Zam was silent as she glared at the Jedi. Finally, she opened her mouth to speak. "It was a bounty hunter called–"

Before she could finish, Zam gasped and then went still. There was a whoosh above them, and the Jedi looked up just in time to see an armored rocket-man disappearing into the sky.

Looking back down, Obi-Wan saw something that he hadn't noticed before: a small, wicked-looking dart lodged in Zam's neck.

After reporting back to the Jedi Council, Obi-Wan and Anakin each took on separate missions. Anakin accompanied Padmé back to Naboo to keep her safe while Obi-Wan set out to track down the rocket-man on his own.

Obi-Wan's first stop was to see an old friend—Dexter Jettster, owner of Dex's Diner and a wellspring of knowledge about the galaxy's underworld.

Obi-Wan showed Dexter the strange dart that had killed Zam Wesell.

"I ain't seen one of these since I was prospecting on Subterrel beyond the Outer Rim!" said Dex. "This baby belongs to them cloners. What you got here is a Kamino saberdart."

Obi-Wan had never heard of Kamino and wondered if the locals would be friendly.

"It depends," Dex replied. "On how good your manners are . . . and how big your pocketbook is."

 To locate Kamino, Obi-Wan went straight to the Jedi Temple's Archives Library.

"Are you sure you have the right coordinates?" asked Madame Jocasta Nu, the Temple's archivist. "It looks like the system you're searching for doesn't exist."

Obi-Wan was sure about the coordinates, all right. So why wasn't Kamino there? He decided to ask one of his old mentors.

Obi-Wan found Yoda teaching a class of Jedi students.

"Lost a planet, Master Obi-Wan has," Yoda announced to his class. "Clear your minds and find Obi-Wan's wayward planet, we will."

The younglings crowded around the star-map reader. Obi-Wan stepped inside the hologram and pointed to where the planet ought to be. "Gravity is pulling all the stars in this area inward to this spot," he said. "There should be a star here . . . but there isn't."

"Most interesting. Gravity's silhouette remains, but the star and all of its planets, disappeared they have. How can this be?" Yoda asked the children.

"Because someone erased it from the archive memory," one boy said. The rest of the children nodded.

"Truly wonderful, the mind of a child is," said Yoda with a chuckle. "Go to the center of gravity's pull, and find your planet you will."

Just as the Jedi younglings had predicted, Obi-Wan found Kamino right where it was supposed to be. Wind and rain lashed his Jedi starfighter as it touched down on the landing platforms of Tipoca City, which was built on stilts above the world's watery surface.

To Obi-Wan's surprise, a tall white alien with almond-shaped eyes greeted him warmly, as if he'd been expected. Taun We led the Jedi to a room bathed in white light.

"The Prime Minister is anxious to see you," she said. "After all these years, we were beginning to think you weren't coming."

ama Su, the Prime Minister of Kamino, greeted Obi-Wan and then said, "Please tell your Master Sifo-Dyas that we have every confidence his order will be met on time. He is well, I hope."

"I'm sorry . . . ," said Obi-Wan, confused. "Sifo-Dyas was killed almost ten years ago."

"Oh, I'm sorry to hear that," Lama Su said. "But I'm sure he would have been proud of the army we've built for him."

"The army?" Obi-Wan asked, now even more confused.

"Yes, a clone army . . . for the Republic."

Lama Su led Obi-Wan to the clone center so he could inspect their progress. Obi-Wan stared at the classrooms filled with boys, all completely identical. In other rooms, older clones dressed in black were eating. Outside, clones in full armor marched in formation in the pounding rain.

According to Lama Su, there were 200,000 troops ready and another million well on their way. Each of them was a perfect clone of one man—a bounty hunter named Jango Fett.

"I would like to meet this Jango Fett," Obi-Wan said.

 **T**aun We took Obi-Wan to Jango's apartment. The door was opened by a boy who looked just like the young clones. But this boy was different. In addition to Jango's considerable pay, he had demanded a clone whose growth would not be accelerated, whom he would raise as a son. His name was Boba.

"Dad! Taun We's here!" Boba called.

Obi-Wan studied the bounty hunter. "Ever make your way as far into the interior of the galaxy as Coruscant?" he asked.

"Once or twice," Jango replied cautiously.

"Recently?" Obi-Wan pressed.

"Possibly. . . ." Jango moved to block Obi-Wan's view of his bedroom. "Boba, close the door," Jango commanded in Huttese.

Boba closed it quickly, but not before Obi-Wan saw several pieces of very familiar body armor lying in the other room.

As soon as the Jedi was gone, Jango turned to his son. "Pack your things," he said. "We're leaving."

17

Meanwhile on Naboo, Anakin was at work on his first important solo mission. Only it didn't feel like work at all! He was guarding Padmé in Naboo's beautiful lake country. They talked and laughed and enjoyed themselves.

Anakin was in love. He had fallen for Padmé the moment he'd first met her ten years ago on Tatooine. And now he suspected that Padmé loved him, too. But there was a problem.

"Jedi aren't allowed to marry," she told him. "You'd be expelled from the Order. I will not let you give up your future for me."

"It wouldn't have to be that way. We could keep it a secret," Anakin suggested. But he felt Padmé was right when she said it could not work. A secret like that could destroy them both.

That night Anakin had a terrible nightmare. He saw visions of his mother. She was suffering and in pain. Anakin knew it was more than a dream. It was a cry for help.

"I know I'm disobeying my mandate to protect you, Senator," said Anakin. "I know I will be punished and possibly thrown out of the Jedi Order. But I have to help her! I don't have a choice."

"I'll go with you," Padmé replied. As long as they were together, he could obey his mandate and continue to protect her.

"What about Master Obi-Wan?" Anakin asked. His Master had ordered him to stay on Naboo.

"I guess we won't tell him, will we?" Padmé said with a smile.

Back on Kamino, Obi-Wan used a transmitter to contact Mace Windu and Yoda on Coruscant.

"I have a strong feeling this bounty hunter is the assassin we're looking for," Obi-Wan reported. He also informed them that Jedi Master Sifo-Dyas had ordered a clone army.

This news worried the Jedi Masters. "Sifo-Dyas did not have the authorization of the Jedi Council," insisted Mace.

"Into custody take this Jango Fett," Yoda instructed Obi-Wan. "Bring him here. Question him, we will."

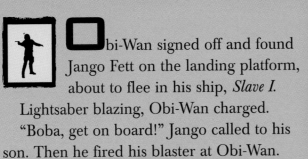

bi-Wan signed off and found Jango Fett on the landing platform, about to flee in his ship, *Slave I.* Lightsaber blazing, Obi-Wan charged. "Boba, get on board!" Jango called to his son. Then he fired his blaster at Obi-Wan.

Obi-Wan deflected the bolts, and Jango used his jetpack to fly over Obi-Wan's head. After landing on a tower, Jango fired again. Then Boba fired shots from the laser cannons on *Slave I,* toppling Obi-Wan and sending his lightsaber skidding across the wet platform.

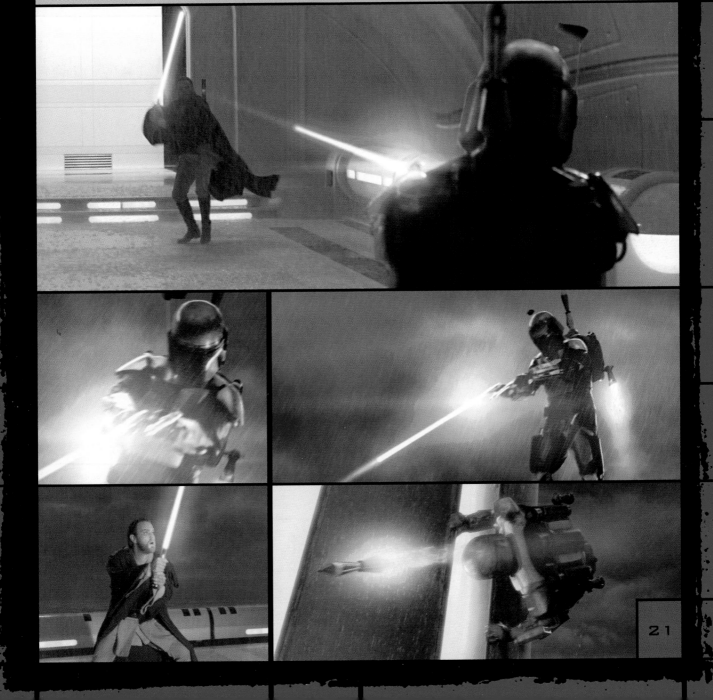

Using the Force, Obi-Wan called his lightsaber to him. But before he could take hold of the hilt, Jango fired a wire from his wrist. It wrapped around Obi-Wan's arms and dragged him across the platform.

With all his strength, Obi-Wan pulled at the wire, jerking Jango to the ground. The bounty hunter's jetpack broke free and exploded. A well-placed Jedi kick sent Jango hurtling toward the platform's edge, but the two were still connected by the wire.

Locked together, they both slid toward the ledge—and a deadly fall.

At the last moment, Jango used the claws on his armor to dig into the curved wall while releasing the wire that tied him to Obi-Wan. Cut loose, Obi-Wan shot right off the platform edge—and toward the raging sea!

Calling upon the Force, Obi-Wan commanded the wire to wrap itself around a pole and stop his fall. By the time he climbed back to the platform, Jango's ship was lifting off.

Thinking fast, Obi-Wan lobbed a small tracking device onto the ship's hull. Then he climbed into his Jedi Delta-7 starfighter and followed *Slave I* into the storm and away from Kamino.

Meanwhile, Anakin returned to Tatooine. When he had last been on this desert planet, he had been a slave. Now his former owner, Watto, hardly recognized him. "A Jedi! Waddya know? Hey, maybe you couldda help me wit some deadbeats who owe me a lot of money," the Toydarian junk dealer suggested.

Anakin had something else in mind. He wanted to find his mother.

"Oh, yeah. Shmi," said Watto. "I sold her."

Years before, a moisture farmer named Cliegg Lars had purchased Shmi to free her from slavery. "Believe it or not, I heard he freed her and married her," Watto explained.

Hearing that the Lars moisture farm was on the other side of Mos Eisley, Anakin and Padmé wasted no time in heading there.

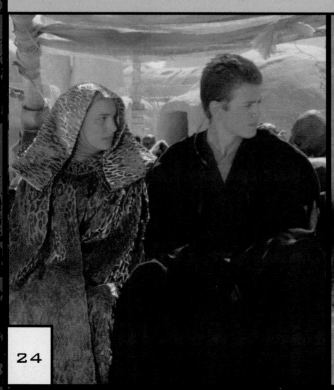

"**O**h, my maker! Master Anakin!" C-3PO could barely contain his excitement. "I knew you would return. I knew you would! And this must be Miss Padmé!"

"I've come to see my mother," Anakin told the Protocol Droid.

C-3PO's excitement faded. "Perhaps we'd better go indoors."

Over steaming cups of ardees, Cliegg Lars, his son, Owen, and Owen's girlfriend, Beru Whitesun, explained that Shmi was not there.

"She was nearby when they took her," Cliegg said sadly, gazing down at his bandaged leg. "Those Tuskens walk like men, but they're vicious, mindless monsters. Thirty of us went out after her. Four of us came back."

There was a heavy silence around the table. Then Anakin stood up.

"Where are you going?" Owen asked.

"To find my mother," Anakin replied grimly.

"Your mother's dead, son. Accept it," Cliegg said.

But Anakin knew she was alive.

Alone, Anakin sped across the harsh desert landscape on Owen's swoop bike. The distances were vast.

At a Jawa encampment, he got a good lead. Still, it took him all day and most of the night to find the Tusken Raiders.

With Jedi stealth, Anakin snuck through their camp. He flattened himself against walls and ducked into shadows. He made his way from hut to hut until he arrived at one that was protected by two guards. The Force told him that this was the one.

After making his way to the back, Anakin quickly cut through the wall with his lightsaber. Inside, he found what he had been looking for: his mother. Anakin quickly cut the ropes that bound her. He gathered her close and cradled his mother's dying body in his arms.

"Mom . . . Mom," he repeated softly.

Shmi's eyes opened a tiny bit. "Annie? Is it you?" she asked.

"I'm here, Mom. You're safe. Hang on. I'm going to get you out of here," Anakin told her.

"My son. My grown-up son. I'm so proud of you, Annie . . . so proud," Shmi whispered. "I missed you so much. . . . Now . . . I am complete."

"Just stay with me, Mom," Anakin pleaded. But it was too late.

"I love . . ." Shmi's body went limp before she could finish.

Gently, Anakin closed her eyes and pulled her closer. He knew his mother was dead.

As the pale light of morning started to grow, Anakin's grief turned to anger and then to hatred.

Overwhelmed by his feelings, Anakin ignited his lightsaber and sought revenge.

The next morning, Anakin returned with his mother's body.

The entire family mourned Shmi's death, but Anakin took it the hardest.

"Why did she have to die? Why couldn't I save her?" Anakin asked Padmé with tears in his eyes.

"Sometimes there are things no one can fix. You're not all-powerful, Annie," Padmé said.

"Well, I should be," he raged. "Someday I will be the most powerful Jedi ever! I promise you, I will even learn to stop people from dying."

Padmé watched as Anakin grew more and more angry. His hands trembled in fury. Padmé sensed that he was upset about more than his mother's death.

"I . . . I killed the Tusken Raiders," Anakin suddenly confessed. "I killed them all." His rage turned back to sorrow as he collapsed into Padmé's arms. Why hadn't he been able to control his anger? Wasn't he a Jedi?

"You're human," Padmé soothed him. "You're like everyone else."

At the small funeral, Anakin stepped forward to kneel beside his mother's grave. Particles of sand slipped through his fingers as he spoke. "I wasn't strong enough to save you, Mom. I wasn't strong enough. But I promise I won't fail again. . . ."

Anakin's throat tightened. He could barely speak. There was so much he wanted to tell his mother, and now he would never have the chance.

"I miss you so much" was all Anakin could say.

eanwhile, Obi-Wan chased Jango Fett's *Slave I* into an asteroid field above the planet called Geonosis. Guiding his Jedi starfighter, Obi-Wan swerved to avoid the sonic charges Jango left in his path.

"He doesn't seem to be able to take a hint," Jango told his son.

"Get him, Dad!" Boba yelled.

The two ships flipped, turned, and rolled—dodging each other and the spinning asteroids. Laser fire clipped Obi-Wan's craft, but it wasn't enough to stop him.

Jango wanted to finish the Jedi off. He pushed a button and launched a guided aerial torpedo. But Obi-Wan had one more trick up his sleeve.

"Arfour, prepare to release the spare-parts containers," Obi-Wan instructed his Astromech Droid. "Release them now!"

Aboard *Slave I*, Boba Fett saw the huge explosion. "Got him!" he cheered.

Sure that their pursuer wouldn't follow them any longer, Jango continued toward the red-rock planet of Geonosis.

Inside his Delta-7 starfighter, on the pitted side of a huge asteroid, Obi-Wan was safe. When he was certain *Slave I* was out of range, Obi-Wan flew toward Geonosis.

Although he'd lost track of exactly where *Slave I* had landed, Obi-Wan found something much more significant—and disturbing. A fleet of Trade Federation starships was hovering above the planet.

I've got to get to the bottom of this, Obi-Wan thought as he approached the fantastic rock-tower buildings on the planet's surface. Inside one of them, he found a suspicious meeting in progress.

From a high balcony, Obi-Wan secretly watched and listened. . . .

"What about the Senator from Naboo?" asked Nute Gunray, the Viceroy of the Trade Federation. "Is she dead yet? I'm not signing your treaty until I have her head on my desk."

"I am a man of my word, Viceroy," Count Dooku coolly assured Nute.

Obi-Wan shook his head in disgust. Now he knew not only *who* had hired assassins to kill Senator Padmé Amidala but *why* they wanted her dead.

It was *revenge,* pure and simple!

Ten years before, when Padmé Amidala had been Queen of Naboo, she had thwarted the Trade Federation's invasion of her planet, making its Viceroy, Nute Gunray, a laughingstock. Now Nute wanted her head.

Obi-Wan listened as Dooku addressed the other officials. Several Senators were there, along with leaders from the Commerce Guilds, the Corporate Alliance, and the InterGalactic Banking Clan. Together they wielded a huge amount of the galaxy's power and wealth.

"Our friends in the Trade Federation have pledged their support," Dooku told them. "When their Battle Droids are combined with yours, we shall have an army greater than anything in the galaxy. The Jedi will be overwhelmed."

Outraged, Obi-Wan turned to leave. He had heard enough. These officials were agreeing to wage a war against the Republic! It was time to contact the Jedi Council.

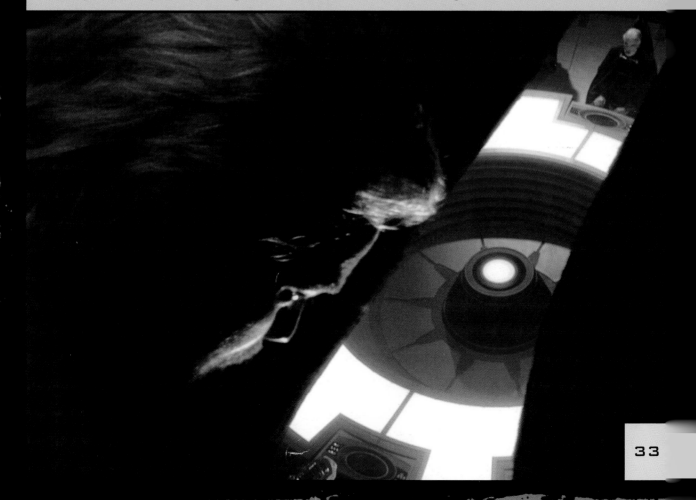

"I have tracked the bounty hunter Jango Fett to the droid foundries on Geonosis. . . ."

Obi-Wan's recorded holographic message flickered in front of Anakin and Padmé on Tatooine.

In the distant Jedi Temple on Coruscant, the Jedi Council also watched the transmitted message.

Everyone listened as Obi-Wan told them what he had learned: The Trade Federation had ordered a new droid army; Viceroy Gunray was behind the assassination attempts on Senator Amidala; and the Commerce Guilds, Corporate Alliance, and InterGalactic Banking Clan were all pledging their droid armies to Count Dooku.

Suddenly, droidekas surrounded Obi-Wan, and his message was cut off!

Count Dooku walked around Obi-Wan in slow circles. The Jedi was helpless, suspended in a crackling blue force field.

"It's a great pity our paths have never crossed before, Obi-Wan," said Dooku. "Qui-Gon always spoke very highly of you. I wish he were still alive. I could use his help."

"Qui-Gon Jinn would never join you," said Obi-Wan of his former Master.

"Don't be so sure, my young Jedi. You forget that he was once my apprentice, just as you were once his. He knew all about the corruption in the Senate. But he would have never gone along with it if he'd known the truth as I have."

"The truth?" Obi-Wan asked.

"The dark side of the Force has clouded their vision, my friend. Hundreds of Senators are now under the influence of a Sith Lord called Darth Sidious."

Obi-Wan shook his head. If the Senate was being manipulated by a Sith Lord, he was sure the Jedi Council would have been aware of it.

"I tried many times to warn them," claimed Dooku, "but they wouldn't listen to me. You must join me, Obi-Wan, and together we will destroy the Sith."

"I will never join you, Dooku."

The Count turned to leave. "It may be difficult to secure your release," he said.

Meanwhile, on Tatooine, Anakin and Padmé were told to stay put by the Jedi Council. The Council would send help to Obi-Wan.

But Anakin and Padmé knew they could get to Obi-Wan faster than the other Jedi. So, with R2-D2 and C-3PO on board, they flew to Geonosis and landed among the red-rock towers.

As they began to look for Obi-Wan, they stumbled upon a droid factory.

"Wait," Anakin said, sensing something he'd missed before. But it was too late. From behind them, winged creatures swooped down to attack.

Anakin's lightsaber blazed in his hand. He cut down several of the creatures, but there were still more. Leaping to another level of the foundry, he battled on.

Padmé fled. With winged Geonosians whirling around her, she barely escaped being caught in the dangerous assembly-line equipment.

Just outside the factory, R2-D2 urged his companion forward.

"If they had needed our help, they would have asked for it," C-3PO had insisted back on the ship. But the little blue droid could not be stopped, and C-3PO followed reluctantly.

Inside the droid factory, R2-D2 spotted Padmé. She was trapped in a vat that was about to be filled with molten metal!

R2-D2 plugged into a port that controlled the vats. Quickly, he reprogrammed the computer. The vat that held Padmé tilted, spilling her to the ground.

Meanwhile, Anakin struggled to free his arm, which had been locked into a molding device that was being slowly drawn toward a sharp cutter. At the last moment, he jerked himself free, saving his arm. But not his lightsaber. The cutter slammed down and split the weapon in two!

Anakin looked up to find himself surrounded by droidekas.

Nearby, Geonosians had trapped Padmé. Suddenly, Jango Fett rocketed in wielding a blaster.

"Don't move, Jedi!" he ordered.

Back on Coruscant, the Senate chamber was in chaos. They had heard the terrible news from Obi-Wan. Count Dooku and his armies were preparing for war! The chair recognized Jar Jar Binks in Senator Amidala's absence, but the Gungan could not speak over the jeering crowd.

"Order!" Mas Amedda yelled. "The Senate will accord the Representative the courtesy of a hearing!" At last the chamber quieted.

"In response to the direct threat to the Republic, meesa propose that the Senate give immediately emergency powers to the Supreme Chancellor," said Jar Jar sheepishly.

The Senate erupted again, this time in applause. Jar Jar beamed and bowed, certain that Senator Amidala would have agreed with his motion. After all, Chancellor Palpatine was such a kind man. Like so many in the Senate, Jar Jar trusted him to do the right thing.

When the applause died, the Chancellor assured the Senate that he'd relinquish his emergency powers as soon as the crisis was over. "And as my first act with this new

authority, I will create a grand army of the Republic to counter the increasing threats of the Separatists," he announced.

On a small balcony overlooking the chamber, Yoda and Mace Windu watched the proceedings. "It is done, then," Mace said. "I will take what Jedi we have left and go to Geonosis to help Obi-Wan."

"Visit I will the cloners on Kamino and see this army they have created for the Republic," Master Yoda replied.

Both Jedi knew that they had witnessed a turning point. But what they had turned toward was still uncertain.

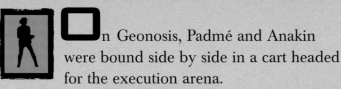

On Geonosis, Padmé and Anakin were bound side by side in a cart headed for the execution arena.

"Don't be afraid," Anakin said.

"I'm not afraid to die," Padmé replied, looking into his eyes. "I've been dying a little bit each day since you came back into my life."

"What are you talking about?"

"I love you," Padmé confessed.

"You love me?" Anakin exclaimed. "I thought that we had decided not to fall in love. That it would destroy our lives."

"I think our lives are about to be destroyed anyway," Padmé pointed out. "I truly, deeply love you, and before we die I want you to know."

Anakin strained against his bindings. His lips touched Padmé's for only a moment before they emerged into the arena.

The stadium was packed with screaming Geonosians. Anakin and Padmé were each chained to a large post standing in the center of the arena. Obi-Wan Kenobi was chained to a third post next to them.

"We decided to come and rescue you," Anakin explained to his Master.

Obi-Wan looked up at his bound hands. "Good job," he said.

Before they could say more, there was a loud announcement: "Let the executions begin!"

Three gates opened to reveal three horrible monsters: a massive bull-like reek, a giant acklay with deadly claws, and a huge nexu with sabers for teeth.

Anakin realized that these would not be ordinary executions. "I've got a bad feeling about this," he said as the reek charged.

Anakin leaped into the air, letting the beast slam into the pole beneath him. Then, landing on its back, Anakin wrapped his chain around the reek's mighty horns. The beast shook its head, tearing the chain free of the post before dancing wildly around the ring. Anakin whirled the chain into the monster's mouth like a bridle and, using the Force, made it obey his direction.

Meanwhile, the acklay was snapping its deadly pincer claws at Obi-Wan, about to slice off the Jedi's head, when Obi-Wan ducked behind his post. SNAP! The creature's claws closed on the post, breaking Obi-Wan's chains and freeing the Jedi!

At the same time, the ferocious nexu roared at Padmé. She had used a wire, which she had hidden, to pick the lock on her hand restraint. Then she had climbed to the top of her post.

Watching from a special box above the arena, Nute Gunray rubbed his hands together in anticipation.

The nexu climbed Padmé's post and took a swipe, tearing the back of her shirt, but she swung around the pole and hit the animal hard on the head with both feet.

"Jump!" someone shouted. It was Anakin. He was directly below her on the reek. Padmé leaped and landed behind him. As they rounded the arena, Obi-Wan jumped up behind his friends.

From above, Nute Gunray scowled. "This is *not* how it is supposed to be! Jango, finish her off!"

"Patience, Viceroy," the Count said. "She will die."

With those words, several droidekas rolled into the arena, surrounding the reek and its riders.

Amid the uproar, Count Dooku did not notice the Jedi visitor in his box until his lightsaber appeared at Jango Fett's neck.

"Master Windu, how pleasant of you to join us," the Count said smoothly.

"Sorry to disappoint you, Dooku," said Mace. "This party's over."

Bolts of light suddenly flashed around the arena as about one hundred Jedi ignited their lightsabers. Yet not even this seemed to upset the Count. "Brave, but foolish, my old Jedi friend. You're impossibly outnumbered."

Suddenly, thousands of Battle Droids flooded in from all sides, and the arena was awash in blaster fire!

Anakin, Obi-Wan, and Padmé jumped off the reek and found weapons.

Mace and several other Jedi leaped to the arena floor.

Jango Fett rocketed after Mace and was nearly trampled by the massive hooves of the now riderless reek. Jango killed the horned monster and turned on the Jedi. But with a single blow, Master Windu proved deadlier than the lethal bounty hunter, and Jango's helmet tumbled across the arena.

At first, the Jedi held their own. Then more droids arrived—Super Battle Droids. The new droids were slow but harder to stop. The Jedi began to fall, and soon the arena was littered with the shattered bodies of droids, Geonosians, and Jedi.

Finally, Mace, Obi-Wan, Anakin, Padmé, and about twenty surviving Jedi stood their ground on the arena floor. These outnumbered few were surrounded by hundreds of Battle Droids and Super Battle Droids.

"Master Windu!" Count Dooku called down. "Surrender—and your lives will be spared."

"We will not be hostages for you to barter with, Dooku," Mace spat back.

"Then I'm sorry, old friend. You will have to be destroyed." Dooku raised his hand, and the droids prepared to fire on his signal.

"Look!" Padmé suddenly shouted. Six Republic gunships descended into the open arena and landed in a cluster around the Jedi. In the doorway of one of the ships stood Yoda.

As clone troopers spilled out to engage the Battle Droids, Obi-Wan, Anakin, and Padmé scrambled aboard one of the gunships, and it lifted out of the arena. The other Jedi retreated in gunships as well. From the air, Mace saw that the arena had been only one small battleground. Ringing the arena were a massive amount of Trade Federation core ships carrying Battle Droids. Flying to meet them head-on were even more Republic assault ships carrying even more clone troopers.

"Hold on!" Obi-Wan suddenly shouted. "Look! Over there . . ."

Anakin turned to see Count Dooku race by in an airspeeder. Quickly, he ordered the pilot of their gunship to follow. On the way, a jolt knocked Padmé out of the gunship, but the Jedi continued to pursue Dooku.

Inside a hangar in a Geonosian tower, Dooku was preparing to leave in his Solar Sailer when Anakin and Obi-Wan rushed in.

"You're going to pay for all of the Jedi you killed today, Dooku," Anakin said angrily.

Beside him, Obi-Wan began to give instructions to his Padawan so they could coordinate their attack, but Anakin would not wait.

"Anakin, no!" Obi-Wan shouted as his Padawan rushed forward with his lightsaber raised.

Dooku watched the young man's charge with a slight smile. At the last moment, Dooku thrust out his arm, using his mastery of the Force to send Anakin flying across the room.

Anakin slammed into the wall and slumped at its foot, barely conscious.

"As you can see, my Jedi powers are far beyond yours," the Count gloated.

"I don't think so," Obi-Wan said, raising his own blade.

Dooku smiled and the lightsaber battle began. It did not take long for Dooku to show himself an expert swordsman. He effortlessly countered Obi-Wan's every move.

"Come, come, Master Kenobi. Put me out of my misery," Dooku taunted.

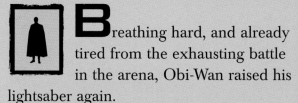

Breathing hard, and already tired from the exhausting battle in the arena, Obi-Wan raised his lightsaber again.

Dooku brought his lightsaber down on Obi-Wan's shoulder, then his thigh. Obi-Wan stumbled. He had reached his limit. He fell.

His lightsaber skittered across the floor. Then he watched as Dooku's lightsaber screamed toward him—and was stopped!

Anakin had thrust his blade under the Count's, saving his Master's life.

Dooku looked Anakin in the eye. "That's brave of you, boy—but foolish," he sneered. "I would have thought you'd have learned your lesson."

Anakin held the Count's gaze. "I'm a slow learner," he replied. Then Anakin attacked, catching the Count off guard and surprising him with his power.

Using the Force, Obi-Wan retrieved his lightsaber and tossed it to Anakin, who now fought the Count using both blades!

Although Anakin had the upper hand for a moment, he could not overcome the Count's skill. Anakin lost one lightsaber. Then in a lightning-fast motion, the Count slashed through Anakin's arm at the elbow and sent the other lightsaber flying—still clutched tightly in the young Jedi's severed fist.

Anakin sank to the ground. Dooku was about to finish him off when through the thick smoke, a small figure emerged. On the threshold stood Master Yoda.

"**Y**ou have interfered with our plans for the last time," Count Dooku told Yoda. Blue Force lightning arced out of his fingertips and toward the tiny Jedi.

The assault was relentless. Yet Yoda stood unfazed. "Much to learn you still have," he said calmly.

Seething, the Count ignited his lightsaber and charged. He attacked ferociously, but Yoda's superior command of the Force prevented Dooku from landing a single blow. Finally, the Count slowed.

Then Yoda attacked. The small but powerful Jedi flew forward, his lightsaber a blur of light. Dooku did not stand a chance against his old Master's magnificent lightsaber skills.

"Fought well you have, my old Padawan," Yoda said when the Count retreated.

"This is just the beginning," Dooku hissed. Using his remaining energy, Dooku sent a giant crane crashing toward Obi-Wan and Anakin.

The two Jedi focused their Force energy to hold the crane back, but it wasn't enough. Quickly, Yoda added his own strength and stopped the crane, saving both Jedi.

It was the distraction Dooku needed to make his escape.

Dooku's Solar Sailer flew to Coruscant and landed in the depths of an abandoned, burnt-out section of the planet.

"The Force is with us, Master Sidious," said Count Dooku to his hooded Sith Master.

"Welcome home, Lord Tyranus. You have done well," Darth Sidious replied.

"I bring you good news, my lord. The war has begun."

Sidious's evil smile showed even in the shadow of his dark cloak. "Excellent," he hissed. "Everything is going as planned."

Meanwhile, high atop the Jedi Temple, Yoda and Mace considered the question that Obi-Wan put to them: "Do you believe what Count Dooku said about Sidious controlling the Senate?"

"Become unreliable, Dooku has. Joined the dark side. Lies, deceit, creating mistrust are his ways now," Yoda replied. "The shroud of the dark side has fallen."

The Jedi agreed they would have to keep a closer watch on the Senate in the future. But Obi-Wan was glad that they had at least been victorious with the help of the clones.

Wise Master Yoda disagreed. "Not victory," the small Jedi said sadly. "Begun, this Clone War has."

Elsewhere on Coruscant, tens of thousands of clone troopers boarded Republic assault ships to wage war throughout the Galaxy.

Back on Padmé's home planet, far from the eyes of the Jedi Masters, Anakin and Padmé stood together on a terrace overlooking a lake. As their droid companions looked on, a Naboo Holy Man blessed the couple's secret union. Then, with a kiss, Anakin and Padmé were married.